This book is dedicated to:

Andréa, Sam, Joseph, Tyler, Alexander,
Ashley, and Haley.

A special thanks to the following people
who helped make this book a reality:
Ellen M. Campbell, Tony Hettinger,
Pam and Nick Horn, Nathaniel Kohlmeier,
Tracy Ramsey, Tanya Sample,
and all the animals on Electra's Acres™.

Christmas 2005

Peyton -
This book was written by a lady
who lives on a farm south of
Fort Wayne. She rescues animals
who need a home. And, she does
have a cow who thinks she is
a horse! She autographed this
book for (maybe she'll be famous
someday).
Love you always,
Grandma

Published by Anton Berkshire Publishing
Printed and bound in the United States

Text ©2003 by Cynthia Mustaine Hettinger
Illustration copyright ©2003 by Jayne Ramsey

Electra's Acres™, Casey the Confused Cow
ISBN 0-9746330-1-1

Casey, the Confused Cow

Cynthia Mustaine Hettinger

Marble, Indiana

Christmas 2005

Written by: Cynthia Mustaine Hettinger

Illustrated by: Jayne Ramsey

Hi, I am Electra and welcome to my farm. All my animal friends live here. One of my friends is a cow named Casey. Casey has one big problem. Casey thinks she is a horse. Casey is very confused because she is not a horse; Casey is a cow. When the other animals on the farm tell her what a lucky cow she is, Casey says, "I do not know anything about cows; I am a horse."

Well, it is true that Casey does not know anything about cows, but Casey is a cow, not a horse. You see, Casey was raised with horses. Her mother was taken to a dairy farm when Casey was very little, so Casey does not remember her mother. Casey has lived with horses all her life, so Casey thinks and acts like a horse.

Casey's best friend is a Welsh pony named
Gertie. Casey and Gertie are always together.
They eat out of the same bowl and sleep in
the same shed. Casey and Gertie are the
best of friends. Because Gertie is a pony,
sometimes the big horses pick on her.
But not when Casey is near. Casey is big.
She weighs more than the biggest horse.
So Casey never lets the other horses pick
on her friend Gertie.

One day the farmer decided that Casey
needed to learn to be a cow. Casey was
sent to another farm to live with cows.

Casey was very sad. She did not like the cows. They complained a lot. The other cows were not very friendly. None of the other cows would share their food bowl with Casey. Casey was so sad that she stopped eating. Casey missed her friend Gertie. Casey missed Electra's Acres.

One day the cow farmer visited the people on Electra's Acres. The cow farmer said that Casey the cow was very sad and would not eat. The cow farmer said he was worried about Casey. So the people on Electra's Acres decided to bring Casey home.

The next day Casey returned to Electra's Acres. She was a very happy cow. Casey was happy to be home. Even the big horses were happy to see Casey. The happiest horse was Gertie the pony. That night Casey and Gertie shared dinner from the same bowl and slept beside each other in the same shed.

The farmer still did not know what to do with Casey. The farmer said, "Casey, cows have calves. Cows provide milk. A cow has a purpose on a farm. You are one confused cow."

Casey just ignored the farmer and rubbed her head against the fence. Casey had an itch.

That night, just before dark, some wild coyotes appeared on Electra's Acres. No one knew where the coyotes had come from.

The alpacas and sheep ran into the barn.
They were very afraid.

The chickens and turkeys ran into the hen
house. They were very afraid.

Coyotes are very mean. The horses and Casey the cow stood in the pasture and watched the coyotes. The mama horse was afraid that the coyotes would hurt her baby.

When Jack and Scout, the farm dogs, saw the coyotes, the dogs tried to chase the coyotes off the farm. But the coyotes were mean and chased the dogs away. Even the brave farm dogs were afraid of the coyotes.

Then the coyotes started to chase the horses. The coyotes were trying to hurt the baby horse.

The horses ran into the corner of the pasture, stopped and faced the mean coyotes. The big horses tried to scare the coyotes away, but they would not leave. The mean coyotes wanted to hurt the baby horse.

The farmer heard the horses holler, and he ran to the pasture. When the farmer saw the coyotes, he ran to the farmhouse to get help. But then something else happened. Casey the cow got mad. She did not like the mean coyotes scaring the horses. Casey did not want her horse friends to get hurt.

So Casey the cow chased the coyotes, and the coyotes ran.

When the farmer and his friends came back to the pasture, they saw the coyotes running away with Casey the cow chasing them.

Everyone cheered. Casey was so brave. Gertie the pony said, "Casey, cows are afraid of coyotes."

"Well," said Casey, "I guess being a confused cow is a good thing because I am not afraid."

"It sure was today," said the big mama horse, "Thank you Casey, for saving my baby."

The farmer scratched Casey's head and said, "Well, I guess you have found your place on the farm. We will no longer call you Casey the confused cow. We will call you Casey the brave cow."

And today you can find Casey on the farm taking her guard duties very seriously, along with eating and sleeping.

The animals on Electra's Acres™:

Casey, the cow

Mariah, Contessa, Gertie, Legacy and Cooper, the horses

Doc, the goat

Travis, Douglas and Nick, the Shetland sheep

Tom, the turkey

The rooster and hens

Lou, Pat, Frank, Echo, David, Red and Paris, the male alpacas

Brita, Socks, Alley, Grace, Ellie and Fortune, the female alpacas

Precious, Austin, Little C, Grayson, Alfalfa, Willie, Madeline, Christopher, Little Bear and Spirit, the cats

Dundee, Indy, Jazz, Pete, Jack, Scout, Dew, Jesse, Ida and Max, the dogs

If you want a photograph of your favorite animal,
send a stamped, self-addressed envelope to:

Electra's Acres™
P.O. Box 372
Markle, IN 46770-0372

Please remember to let us know who your favorite animal is.

Visit our Web site
www.electrasacres.com